MERRY Christmas "1997"
From: The Roudebush Family

Paddington's Magical Christmas
Text copyright © 1988 by Michael Bond.
Illustrations copyright © 1993 by HarperCollins Publishers Ltd.
First published in Great Britain by William Collins Sons and Co Ltd.
This edition published in 1993 by HarperCollins Publishers Ltd.
Printed and bound in Hong Kong
❖
First American Edition, 1993.

Library of Congress Cataloging-in-Publication Data
Bond, Michael.
   Paddington's magical Christmas / by Michael Bond ; illustrated by
John Lobban.
      p.   cm.
   Summary: When he hears members of the Brown household singing
"The Twelve Days of Christmas," Paddington gets confused and
thinks they are receiving unusual presents that keep disappearing be-
fore he can see them.
   ISBN 0-694-00503-7
   [1. Bears—Fiction.   2. Christmas—Fiction.   3. Twelve days of
Christmas (English folk song)—Fiction.]   I. Lobban, John, ill.   II. Ti-
tle.
PZ7.B6368Pank   1993   92-41745
[E]—dc20   CIP
                                                               AC

Paddington's
Magical Christmas

Michael Bond

Illustrated by John Lobban

HarperFestival
A Division of HarperCollinsPublishers

One day, not long before Christmas, Paddington was busy doing his homework when he heard Mrs. Bird singing, which was very unusual.

As he listened to the words, he nearly fell off his chair with surprise. It seemed her true love had sent her a present of a partridge in a pear tree.

He hurried into the garden, but to his disappointment there were no pear trees to be found, let alone one with a partridge in it.

He gazed hopefully at Mr. Brown's apple tree, but, except for a few sparrows and a robin redbreast, the branches were bare.

As soon as Paddington came back inside, he heard Mrs. Brown singing that *her* true love had sent four calling birds, three French hens, two turtle doves, and another partridge in a pear tree.

Paddington could hardly believe his ears. He rushed back out to the garden.

Once again he was too late. Even the sparrows and the robin redbreast had flown away. The only bird left was a fat old pigeon sitting on the lawn.

This time, Paddington was determined to keep his eyes and ears open. Clearly something was going on.

Sure enough, no sooner had he come back inside than it was Judy's turn to break into song.

This time she announced that in addition to the four calling birds, three French hens, two turtle doves, and a partridge in a pear tree, she had been given five gold rings.

Paddington decided that the Browns must have some very rich friends if they could afford so many presents. It made his own list seem very small.

Over the next few days the mystery deepened.

Six geese a-laying arrived, along with seven swans a-swimming, but they all disappeared before Paddington had a chance to see them. He even tried looking in the oven, but Mrs. Bird drove him out of the kitchen with her feather duster.

Eight maids a-milking came and went, and all that Paddington found was a note on the front doorstep asking for "two extra pints, please."

When Paddington heard what Mrs. Bird sang next—nine ladies dancing—he decided that perhaps she had ordered the extra milk in case they got thirsty. He searched the house from top to bottom, but there was no sign of anybody. Then, just as he was coming downstairs, he heard Jonathan singing. It seemed that he had been sent no less than ten lords a-leaping. Everyone was receiving such unusual presents!

Paddington decided to go and see his friend, Mr. Gruber, who had an antique shop on Portobello Road. Mr. Gruber had piles of books about every subject under the sun, and Paddington felt sure he would be able to explain the mystery.

"Tell me, Mr. Brown," he said. "What is the problem? I can see you are very worried about something."

"Something strange is going on," said Paddington. "The Browns and Mrs. Bird have been receiving all kinds of Christmas presents, like exotic birds and gold rings. But before I can have a peek, everything disappears."

Mr. Gruber listened carefully as Paddington told him the whole story.

"I think, Mr. Brown," he said at last, "that if you were to go back home you would probably find eleven pipers piping as well."

Paddington gazed at Mr. Gruber in astonishment.

"You see, Mr. Brown," he explained, "they haven't really been getting presents. They have all been singing a Christmas carol. But you have given me an idea for *your* present. We'll have to hurry, though. It's Christmas Eve and the stores will be closing early."

With Paddington trying to keep up, Mr. Gruber led the way down Portobello Road. As they weaved through the stalls lining the street, Mr. Gruber explained what he had in mind.

Paddington grew more and more excited as he listened. "Just leave it to me," said Mr. Gruber. "I think that with the help of some of our friends in the market, we will be able to give everyone a Christmas to remember."

Mr. Gruber was as good as his word, and on Christmas morning, right after breakfast, a very strange procession began making its way from the market toward number thirty-two Windsor Gardens.

On the twelfth day of Christmas my true love sent to me

Twelve drummers drumming . . .

Eleven pipers piping . . .

Ten lords a-leaping . . .

Nine ladies dancing . . .

Eight maids a-milking . . .

Seven swans a-swimming . . .

Six geese a-laying . . .

Five gold rings . . .

Four calling birds . . .

Three French hens . . .

Two turtle doves . . .

And a partridge in a pear tree . . .

"If you ask me," said Mrs. Bird, as she invited everyone in for hot mincemeat pies, "that is the nicest Christmas morning anyone could possibly wish for. But then," she added, "with a bear like Paddington around, life is always full of lovely surprises."